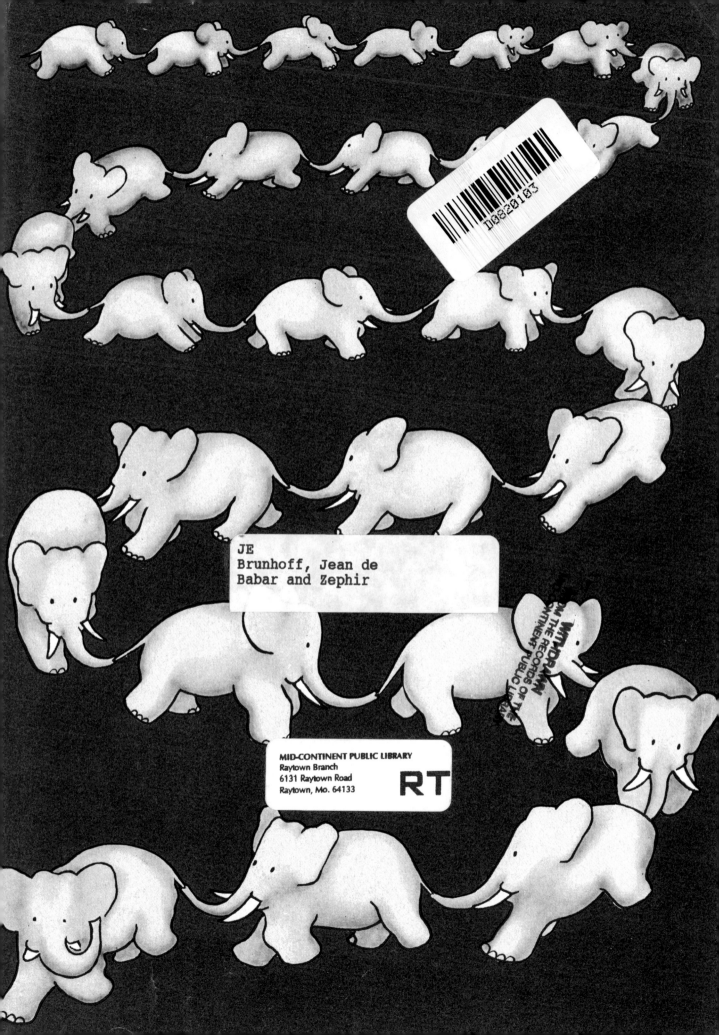

JEAN DE BRUNHOFF

BABAR AND ZEPHIR

Translated from the French by Merle S. Haas
Random House 🏠 New York

JEAN DE BRUNHOFF'S

Babar Books

The Story of Babar

The Travels of Babar

Babar the King

Babar and Zephir

Babar and His Children

Babar and Father Christmas

Bonjour, Babar!
(Compilation with an introduction by Kevin Henkes)

www.randomhouse.com/kids

Library of Congress Cataloging-in-Publication Data
Brunhoff, Jean de, 1899–1937.
Babar and Zephir / Jean de Brunhoff ; translated from the French by Merle S. Haas.
p.   cm.
Originally published in slightly different form: [New York] : Random House, c1937
under the title Zephir's holidays. Also published under the title Babar's friend, Zephir.
SUMMARY: While on summer vacation, Babar's monkey friend, Zephir,
goes fishing and accidentally catches a mermaid, then enlists
her aid in saving Princess Isabelle, who has been kidnapped by a horned monster.
ISBN 0-394-80579-8 (trade) — ISBN 0-394-90579-2 (lib. bdg.)
[1. Monkeys—Fiction.   2. Mermaids—Fiction.   3. Kidnapping—Fiction.]
I. Haas, Merle.   II. Title.
PZ7.B828428 Babbf 2002 [E]—dc21 2002069738

Printed in the United States of America   10 9 8 7 6 5 4 3 2 1

First jacketed hardcover edition

The elephants' school at Celesteville is closed for the whole summer. Zephir, the little monkey, as well as his bigger schoolmates, goes off for the holidays. What fun to go and see his family again! But how sad to leave his friends, King Babar, Queen Celeste, the Old Lady, his teacher, and his beloved Arthur!

All four have promised to come to the river near the bridge to see him off and bid him a last fond farewell. There they are. Zephir catches sight of them. He waves his handkerchief and calls out: "Au revoir!"

Zephir arrives at the station of Monkeyville
and throws himself into his mother's arms.

"Gracious! How you've grown, my darling!"
she says, as she kisses him on both cheeks.

Everybody has piled into the family car. Zephir rides in front next to his father; his mother rides in back with his little sister and his brothers.

"Let's go! Step on the gas!" says Zephir.

They have to use a rope
ladder to climb up to the
house perched there in the
treetops. Zephir scrambles up
easily, but laughs as he says
to himself: "This wouldn't
do at all for my friends the
elephants."

The house is small but comfortable. While his mother prepares a good soup of bananas and chocolate, Zephir plays hide and seek with his brothers. His father carries up the baggage, and little sister swings to and fro.

Zephir falls asleep almost as soon as his head touches the pillow. But in the middle of the night, the nightingale wakes him with his song: "Trou-lala, tiou-tiou-tiou! Tidi! Tidi!"

Zephir gets up gaily, and runs to the window. "Hello, old chap!"

The two cronies now have a little chat.

"Do you know what? There's a big package for you at the station," says the nightingale breathlessly. "On the label is written: 'From Babar'."

"Maybe it's a piano," answers Zephir. "I won first prize in music, you know."

Next morning Zephir hurries to the station. What a wonderful surprise! King Babar has sent him a real rowboat. Zephir, with his father's help, rolls it into the water.

He's going in for a swim, and then later will fish. The elephants have

taught him how. The monkeys admire his courage, for they themselves
are afraid of the water.

Princess Isabelle, turning to her father, General Huc, says: "Oh, what
a daredevil that fellow Zephir is!"

"What's this I've caught?" Zephir asks himself, greatly surprised. And then the beautiful creature speaks:

"Oh, Mr. Monkey," she says, "don't squeeze me so hard; you're choking me. Listen to me, I pray. I'm a tiny little mermaid, and live in the sea. I have a head and arms, just like you; but see, I have a fish's tail. I'm accustomed to my life in the ocean waves. If you carry me off into the forest, I'll surely die. Leave me here to swim about with my sisters. My name is Eléonore. Maybe, some day, you'll have need of me. If so, throw three pebbles into the water, and repeat my name three times. No matter where I am, I'll hear you and come to you. I will never forget you."

Zephir listens to the mermaid, and then gently frees her from the fish hook. He has just let her go, but is a little sad at having lost her.

On his way home, Zephir sees some monkeys reading the newspapers in the street, and hears the newsboy shouting: "Extra! Extra! Princess Isabelle vanishes!"

"Poor little thing," thinks Zephir. "It can't be true! She was on the beach this morning when I started out to fish."

He listens to the passers-by, and this is what he hears: Isabelle was playing in the palace gardens, when suddenly she was surrounded by a green cloud which wrapped itself around her, hiding her from her friends. Then the cloud rose, leaving behind it a strong odor of rotting apples. The princess hadn't been seen since.

General Huc, full of anxiety and despair, calls out his guardsmen, and gives Colonel Aristobald his orders.

"General," this brave officer replies, "I promise we will do our very best to find your daughter, the princess."

By air, by water, from the treetops and the mountain peaks, even through the underbrush, Aristobald and his soldiers hunt for the princess. In spite of all their efforts, they find no trace of her.

General Huc arrives in his car to get the latest news. When ques-
tioned, the colonel lowers his head sadly. The general understands what
this means, and goes away with a heavy heart.

Zephir is the only one who doesn't give up hope. Secretly, he puts a gourd and some provisions into his knapsack. He also takes with him his most prized possessions: his violin and his clown costume. Then he starts off toward the sea. Luckily the beach is deserted. He picks up three pebbles, throws them into the water and calls out three times: "Eléonore, my friend, Zephir awaits you here!"

Instantly, just as she had promised, the little mermaid appears.

"Isabelle is lost! Can you help me find her?" asks Zephir.

"That will be difficult," she answers. "But for your sake I'm willing to try. Wait here; I'll go and get my carriage."

A few minutes later Zephir is happily seated in a gigantic sea-going shell. They are off! The racing fish pull them along speedily. Eléonore guides them toward a wild-looking island, and points it out, saying: "That's where my Aunt Crustadele lives. Let's visit her in her grotto; she will give us good advice."

"My children," said Crustadele, after listening to them in silence, "he who smells of rotting apples, he who carried off Isabelle, must be Polomoche."

"Who is Polomoche?" asks Zephir.

"He is a monster who lives on his island with his friends the Gogottes. They live on herbs and fruits, and are not savage. But they are bored.

"From time to time, in order to amuse himself, Polomoche goes off for a trip in a little green cloud. If he meets anyone he likes, he carries him off to his cave. That's what has happened to Isabelle. He is capricious, impatient, and has a bad habit of turning to stone those who anger him.

"Little monkey, if you want to save your princess, there's not a moment to lose. Eléonore will drive you there and wait for you. Take this old sack; it will prove useful.

"And remember, in order to succeed, you'll have to make Polomoche laugh. You'll recognize him by his pointed horns and his yellow skin.

"Leave at once, and good luck to you!"

After a good crossing, Eléonore and Zephir
land without being seen by the Gogottes. The
country looks bleak. They are now silently taking
leave of each other. Zephir holds his friend's
little hand in his own.

Zephir puts on Crustadele's sack. It covers
him and his few belongings completely, and he
immediately resembles the rocks which are
scattered all over the island. He walks cautiously
to the top of the hill, while working out his plans.

When he gets to the top, he hears a gruff voice. Quickly removing the sack, he peeks through the rocks. There is Isabelle, right in the midst of the monsters!

"Little monkey," growls Polomoche, "I carried you off because I thought you'd be amusing, and here you do nothing but cry! I've had enough of this. I'm going to change you into a rock!"

"Lord Polomoche, and you, Ladies and Gentle-men, permit me to salute you!" says the brave Zephir, politely, as he suddenly emerges from behind the rocks. "I am a clown-musician by pro-fession. Pray allow me to stop here a while, to try to entertain you."

Isabelle, recognizing him, drops her hand-kerchief and thinks to herself: "Ah! He has come just in the nick of time!"

Pretty soon, thanks to Zephir, everyone is at ease. A pleasant air of gaiety prevails. He tells them stories: one about the rat with an elephant's trunk; one about the blind huntsman; one about Captain Hoplala and the gun made of macaroni; and one about Percefeuille and Filigrane. Each time he finishes a tale, Polomoche and the Gogottes cry: "Tell us another! Tell us one more!"

Tired of talking, Zephir now dons his clown costume. What luck to have brought it with him!

"Presto!"

"There he is!"

"I'm now going to show you a game, 'the chase of the magic hat'."

Having said these words, Bang! Crash! he falls down and turns several somersaults at top speed, and then, when he catches his hat with his tail, Polomoche bursts out laughing heartily.

"That's fine!" thinks the crafty Zephir. "One more little stunt, and the time will be ripe for action. My plan is a good one. By tomorrow we will be far away."

Then, picking up his violin, he plays waltzes and polkas, one after the other. Carried away by the music, they all jump and whirl about giddily.

At last, tired out, they all roll over in a heap and go to sleep, and start to snore peacefully. Zephir takes off his costume and prepares to escape.

"The moment has come!" he whispers to Isabelle, and they dash off to the sea, as fast as their legs can carry them. Eléonore is waiting and waves to them.

They are saved! Land is in sight!

On their way back they stop to thank Crustadele. Some
birds have announced their return, and the news travels fast.
Polomoche and the Gogottes sleep on.

The monkeys come running from all directions. Some
run down to the beach, others watch from the cliff. General
Huc takes out his spy-glass. Zephir's family cries for joy.

Zephir and Isabelle are warmly greeted by the enthusiastic crowd, who shower them with flowers. They've said good-by to the gentle Eléonore, who has gone back home with her fish.

The general congratulates Zephir in front of the soldiers of his guard, and says: "My young friend, I, General Huc, President of the Republic of the Monkeys, am proud of you, and give you my beloved daughter, Isabelle. You may marry her later on, when you become of age."

After this ceremony, when Zephir goes home, his father and his mother, his sister and his brothers, all make a big fuss over him too. They are so happy to see him again that they don't scold him for having gone off without telling them and causing them so much concern. They dance around with him and sing: "Long live the betrothed!"

After starting off with this astonishing adventure, the rest of the holidays pass peacefully and happily. Zephir goes back to Celesteville. As long as he lives with the elephants, Eléonore and her sisters will watch over Isabelle.

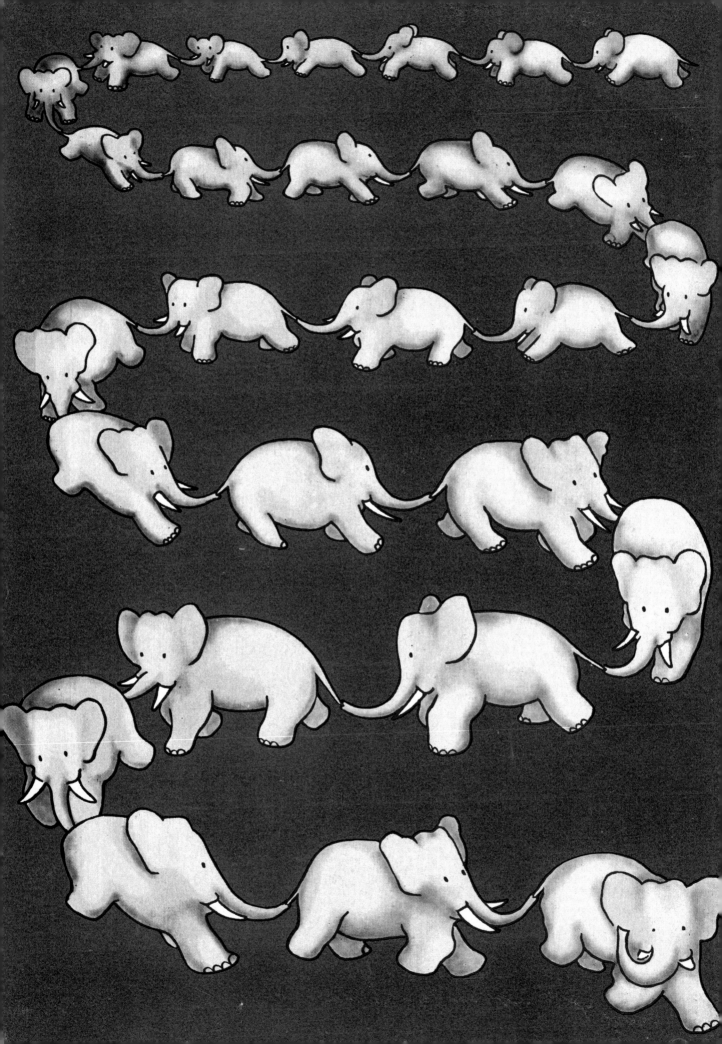